The Littlest Elf

Written by
Brandi Dougherty

Illustrated by
Kirsten Richards

Cartwheel Books
An imprint of Scholastic Inc.

For Annette, Gina, and Nicole
—B.D.

For Scott and Matt, the cheekiest elves I know
— K.R.

Text copyright © 2012 by Brandi Dougherty.
Illustrations copyright © 2012 by Kirsten Richards.
Library of Congress Cataloging-in-Publication Data is available

All rights reserved. Published by Scholastic Inc.
SCHOLASTIC, CARTWHEEL BOOKS, and associated logos are trademarks and/or registered trademarks of Scholastic Inc.

ISBN 978-0-545-48978-2

10 9 8 7 6 5 4 3 2 1   12 13 14 15 16

Printed in the U.S.A.   40
First printing, September 2012

Oliver was an elf.
He lived with his family in the North Pole.
There were many elves in Santa's Village,
but Oliver was the littlest one.

It was Christmastime and Oliver was excited.
This year he would discover his special job at one of Santa's workshops.

Bicycle Workshop

Bakery

Bookmakers

Toy Workshop

He just needed to visit each shop to see which one was the right fit.

At the toy workshop where his mom worked,
Oliver tried to make cuddly teddy bears.
But he got lost in the huge stuffing pile!
"Oliver?" an elf asked.

Oliver's mom said, "I think you're too little for the toy workshop. Why don't you try helping your dad at the bicycle workshop instead?"

So Oliver went to Santa's bicycle workshop.
"I'm ready to help!" he said.
Oliver watched as the elves added wheels
and seats and handlebars and bells.

But the tools were very big for Oliver's little hands.
"Maybe baking is your special job," Oliver's dad told him. "You should visit your brother at the bakery next."

Off Oliver went to the bakery.
These elves made sugarplum cookies and candy cane squares!
But when Oliver tried to stir the cookie dough…
"Oliver, look out!" one of the elves shouted.

He fell into a giant mixing bowl.
"Sorry, Ollie," his brother said. "You're too little for the bakery.
Maybe your special job is at the bookmakers' shop."

Oliver arrived at the last of Santa's workshops, where his sister worked. The bookmakers there wrote amazing stories and drew wonderful pictures.
"Can I help?" Oliver asked.
"Of course!" the elves replied.

But the inkpot was kind of tough to reach ... and the stack of paper was very tall.
"Oh, Ollie!" his sister cried.
Bookmaking was harder, and messier, than it looked.

Oliver wandered through the North Pole.
He was sad.
Oliver knew there had to be one special
job he could do, even if he was little.

Then he heard the sound of hooves clattering at the stables.
Inside, a herd of reindeer had gathered to meet Dot, the new reindeer.
She was little, just like Oliver.

Dot was very excited to help fly Santa's sleigh.

She practiced for the big night by jumping and hopping

and leaping,

but she could not fly.

The reindeer's mama gave her a gentle kiss.
Dot was still too little.

Dot looked very sad.

Oliver wanted to cheer her up. He dug in his pockets to find a treat for Dot, but instead he found little trinkets from each workshop he had visited. Just then, he had an idea!

Oliver and Dot used the tiny treasures to make ornaments, cards, and fun decorations for all the hardworking elves in the village.

The littlest elf and the littlest reindeer filled a sleigh with their Christmas treats. They delivered the presents to all the workshops. The elves loved their special gifts.

Soon, Santa came to see what all the fuss was about.
He watched as Oliver and Dot made everyone smile.

Suddenly, Santa had an idea. "Oliver and Dot," he said, "with your big hearts and great Christmas cheer, won't you be my very important helpers this year?"

Oliver and Dot had found their
special jobs after all!
But more important, they had
each found a special friend!